I0816860

ON A VINEYARD VERANDA

Limericks by **MOLLY MANLEY**

Illustrations by **JANET MARSHALL**

COMMONWEALTH EDITIONS
Beverly, Massachusetts

To Rick and Debbie, George and Gloria, John and Kerrie

M. H. M.

To Christine, Kelly, Alex, Robby, Will, Andrew, Joseph, Jayson, Tate, Thomas, Tyler, and Marlon

J. P. M.

ISBN-13: 978-1-933212-46-3
ISBN-10: 1-933212-46-2

Library of Congress Cataloging-in-Publication Data
Manley, Molly (Molly Hollingworth)
On a vineyard veranda / limericks by Molly Manley ; illustrations by Janet Marshall.
p. cm.
ISBN-13: 978-1-933212-46-3 (alk. paper)
ISBN-10: 1-933212-46-2 (alk. paper)
1. Limericks. 2. Martha's Vineyard (Mass.)—Poetry. I. Title.

PN6231.L5M3745 2007
811'.54—dc22
2007001808

Printed in Korea

Commonwealth Editions is an imprint of Memoirs Unlimited, Inc.,
266 Cabot Street, Beverly, Massachusetts 01915.
Visit us on the Web at www.commonwealtheditions.com

A cream puff from Oak Bluffs, Raquel,
Loved to ride on the old carousel.
Her most thrilling thing
Was to catch the brass ring
And have tea at the Wesley Hotel.

A surfer superb from Squibnocket
Zoomed over the waves like a rocket,
So her mom thought it best
That she wear a life vest
And keep a cell phone in her pocket.

Three Edgartown swingers named Bates,
Known for singing and swinging on gates,
Would not sing at night
For it wasn't polite,
And their bedtime came well before eight.

A cyclist from Moshup named Minna
Who biked to the cliffs of Aquinnah
Became frightened of heights
While admiring the sights
And believed that she might lose her dinner.

25¢

TURP

A West Tisbury maid, merry May,
Painted pictures of daisies all day.
Then she painted a barn
At the old Allen Farm
And relaxed with a game of croquet.

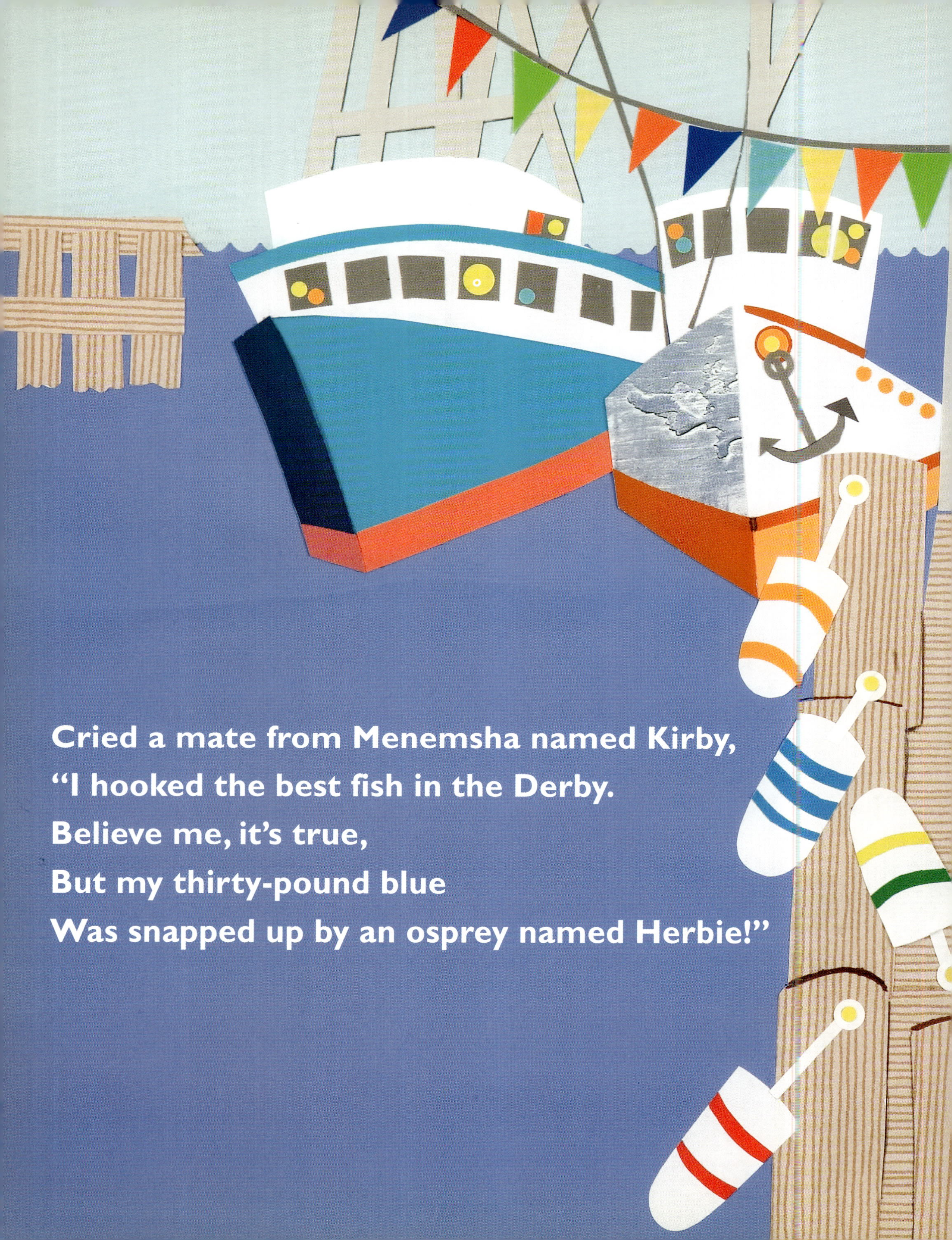

Cried a mate from Menemsha named Kirby,
"I hooked the best fish in the Derby.
Believe me, it's true,
But my thirty-pound blue
Was snapped up by an osprey named Herbie!"

One day at South Beach, naughty Donna
Threw mud pies and then pinched her mama.
Dumping sand in her hair,
She ran around bare.
Oh, what an embarrassing drama!

A crew from the yacht club, quite snappy,
Went aground around Wasque, off Chappy.
They jumped ship at once,
And then the whole bunch
Ferried home right "On-Time" and quite happy.

At the street fair in fair Vineyard Haven,
A dude known for rude misbehavin'
Hurled water balloons
On a hot afternoon,
Raising havoc and waterlogged mayhem.

A lickety-splitter named Chase
Took a spill in the Chilmark road race.
He scraped both his knees
By the Beetlebung trees
But still managed to take second place.

0
1

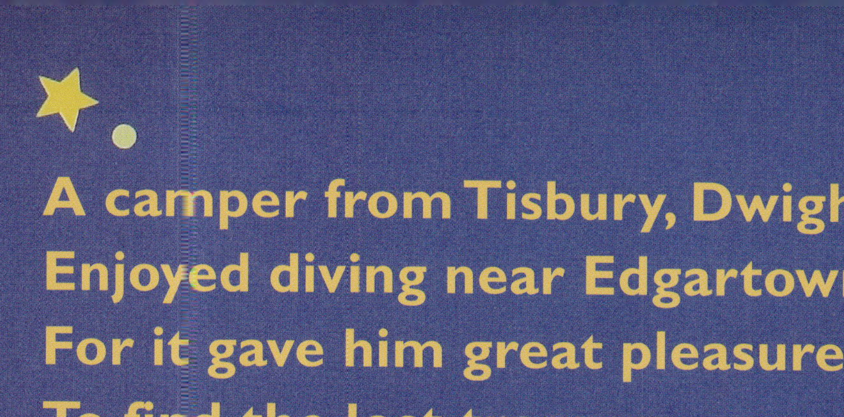

A camper from Tisbury, Dwight,
Enjoyed diving near Edgartown Light,
For it gave him great pleasure
To find the lost treasure
That went out with the tide every night.

On her Vineyard vacation, Amanda
Loved to sleep on her grandma's veranda.
On 'Lumination Night
With the lanterns alight
Not a place in the world could be grander.